The Briny Deep Mysteries

THE DISAPPEARING

The Briny Deep Mysteries Book 1

Jennifer Torres

Speeding Star

I'm thankful for so many things.

A late night chat years ago under a sea of stars when my son Timmy and I began to dream up a story about a place called Briny Deep.

My daughter Emily who believed in the story and told me to write it now because the laundry could wait.

*My daughter Isabelle who agreed (begrudgingly) to take a break from her Movie Star Planet computer game so I could actually use **my** computer to write.*

A horrible boss and soul zapping job that made me realize I had to send out what I wrote because my dreams were not going to come find me.

My editors: David Dilkes for believing in me and being the original champion for this story—and the funny, patient, inspiring David Mulrine for all the pep talks and ego boosting emails.

Supportive family members like my dear mother for reading each and every word the minute I wrote it, my Dad, Jim, Danny, Stacey, Matthew, and my sister Natalie.

And finally to my wonderful husband—and fellow dream chaser—John, who refused to hear any more of my "great book ideas" until I actually wrote one to completion. I love you.

Library of Congress Cataloging-in-Publication Data

Torres, Jennifer.

    The disappearing / Jennifer Torres.

        pages cm. — (The Briny Deep mysteries ; book 1)

        Summary: "Tim, Max, Emily, Luke, and Nina learn that their quiet town of Briny Deep isn't as safe as they once thought. With children vanishing, they need to find answers before all their friends disappear"—Provided by publisher.

    ISBN 978-1-62285-172-0

    [1. Mystery and detective stories. 2. Missing children—Fiction. 3. Friendship—Fiction. 4. Science fiction.] I. Title.

    PZ7.T645648Di 2014

    [Fic]—dc23   2014000875

Future editions:

Paperback ISBN: 978-1-62285-173-7   EPUB ISBN: 978-1-62285-174-4

Single-User PDF ISBN: 978-1-62285-175-1   Multi-User PDF ISBN: 978-1-62285-176-8

Speeding Star
Box 398, 40 Industrial Road
Berkeley Heights, NJ 07922
USA
www.speedingstar.com

Cover Illustration: © Johan Swanepoel/Shutterstock.com

Contents

Chapter 1

A Midnight Visit

Every night Tim runs for his life.

Through a sticker bush, onto a dirt path, his lungs straining for air as he pushes ahead down a small hill.

Faster now.

The man pursuing him is close; he can hear twigs snap under heavy feet, pounding into the grass just behind him. Ahead, a patch of flowers and a yellow house, if he can just get there, but then he remembers he won't make it.

He never does.

The rock, hidden in the grass, is steps away. Tim trips, landing on his knees, a strong hand grips his shoulder, pulling him away again.

It was a nightmare he could do without.

Yet here he was again, sitting straight up in bed, sweaty, gasping for air, forced out of a sound sleep at the same moment in the dream every time.

"Whew," he exhaled. Lying back down with hands clasped behind his head, Tim silently considered telling his mom he might need to talk to someone about this. The whole thing was getting ridiculous already.

Soon enough his eyes grew heavy, his breathing deep, then . . .

BANG—BANG—BANG!

Tim jumped to his feet. Someone was here, and they wanted in.

Within moments, he could hear his parents' bedroom door swing open, their feet moving quickly down the steps. In his head, one thought screamed out:

Don't open it!

Tim slipped out his door, into the hallway, and peered down the staircase just in time to see his father open the front door.

It was the police.

"Sorry to bother you at this hour, but there's been an incident," said a giant, burly man with dark eyes. "Can we talk for a moment?"

"Tim?" his mom called out as she made her way up the stairs.

"I'm right here," he quickly stammered and ran to meet her half way. "What's wrong, Mom? What happened?"

She threw her arms around her son and exhaled in relief, "I don't know, I don't know."

As his father led the man inside, Tim's mother walked him to his room, making sure he was safely back in bed. Then she slipped back down the stairs to join the others.

He could hear the door to his father's study click shut, and then nothing.

Soon he drifted off into a mercifully uneventful sleep.

≈≈≈≈≈

"Did you hear what happened last night?" asked Max as he rode up on his skateboard the next morning. "Everyone is talking about it."

"Yeah, they came to my house in the middle of the night to tell my parents," said Tim, who had been sitting on the steps of his front porch waiting for his friend Max. "They told me this morning."

He stood up, jumped on his own board, and the two headed down the road to the beach sharing what details they had.

All they really knew was that a young girl in town had disappeared. Her name was Eva. Everyone knew her and liked her. Her parents were inconsolable and certain she had been taken by a stranger—a man Eva told her mother she had seen just days earlier.

"A stranger in Briny Deep?" said Max. "Now *that's* strange."

Nothing bad ever happened in Briny Deep.

Tim had lived here all his life and couldn't imagine a better place to grow up. Nestled in the hills, crested by the sea, he spent his days at the beach, playing ball, and hanging out with his four best friends.

They had known each other forever. It helped that all their parents were friends, too. They were always at each other's houses for barbecues, pool parties, and movie nights. It might have been difficult if their kids hadn't got along. But luckily the friendships came easily and instantly and were fiercely strong, even though two of his best friends were girls.

Nina and Emily were always together and thought of each other like sisters. And Tim and the guys, Luke and Max, were brothers in every sense of the word but blood. They even wore these silly matching fabric bands around their wrists. They had made them one summer at camp—when they were much younger. Emily teasingly referred to them as their "friendship bracelets."

Everyone at school called the five of them "The Family," which would have been okay except for the fact that Tim had feelings for Nina that went a bit beyond friendship.

As much as he tried to deny these feelings and push them aside, they persisted.

"Hey," Nina called out as she rolled up behind him on her board, causing Tim to nearly fall off of his.

"Hey back," he managed to reply.

She smiled and gazed up at him with those eyes, "I thought we could ride over together."

"Uh, am I invisible here?" Max shouted as he fell onto the pavement in a failed attempt ride the curb.

Laughing, Nina jumped off her board, ran over to Max, and began playfully tousling his hair. "You are too good looking to be invisible."

Tim suddenly felt like throwing up.

The three jumped back on their boards and headed to the shore.

Paradise Beach was packed.

It seemed as though the entire school was there, hoping to catch a few more rays of sun before school started again next week. Someone had plastered posters all over town, encouraging everyone to come out for one last summer party on the beach—and it appeared everyone had.

Barbecues were being manned across the park leading down to the sand. Thick, sweet smoke filled the air as meat sizzled on dozens of grills. Younger kids ran past, heading for the playground, fingers and faces sticky with remnants of quickly devoured ice cream. Several volleyball games were in full swing, and kites filled the air.

Emily and Luke spotted them first and quickly darted through the crowd to meet them.

Emily looked nervous. "Did you hear what happened?"

Nope, nothing bad ever happened in Briny Deep, until the stranger arrived.

Chapter 2

The Search for Eva

A warm gust of ocean air purred through Tim's hair as he raced his friends past throngs of beachgoers, searching for an unoccupied patch of sand.

Luke's call was barely a whisper over the pounding waves as they crashed on shore. "Over here!"

The group met up on what had to be the last free spot on the beach and proceeded to set up for the day. Luke and Emily had brought along a beach blanket, chairs, and a cooler full of icy drinks.

"Emily, I'm over here!" a little voice called from nearby.

It was Isabelle, Emily's little sister and practically her twin in appearance—but a mini-size version. She was three years younger. The two were extremely close—they even shared a "Best Friends" necklace. It was a heart that was broken in half with the inscription *Best Friends Forever* on it. Each sister wore one half around her neck.

"Okay, Izzy, just don't go too far, alright?"

Isabelle put her thumb up in agreement and ran off with her friends.

The boys had already continued on toward the shore, where they dove into the cold blue water with zeal.

Nina grabbed a juice from the cooler and moved a tray of brownies Emily had made to a shadier spot of blanket.

"Perfect day," Emily purred, stretching her arms up over her head. "It's so sad school has to start again so fast. I can't stand to be cooped up when the weather is so perfect."

Nina sprawled out on the blanket, letting the hot sun wash over her skin. She squinted and peered over her shoulder at Emily.

Her curly, platinum blonde hair glistened in the light. Her skin was milky. She was a dancer, which made her graceful and fit. She always dressed as if she was attending an event in her honor, with her makeup perfect, her shoes the latest style. But for all her obvious beauty and elegance, she was even more beautiful inside. Smart, kind, and compassionate, she had listened for hours—over too many nights to count—as Nina spilled her heart out over the way she felt about Tim.

Nina was thankful she had finally let go of all that and moved on. Tim didn't feel the same about her—it was obvious. But he was one of her best friends, and she would never risk losing that over some stupid crush.

In contrast to Emily, Nina's long, straight hair was dark brown, almost black. She often scooped it up in a ponytail. Her olive skin tanned easily, and while she was often called beautiful by her friends, she preferred T-shirts and cutoffs to designer clothes. She dreaded shopping for shoes and purses. Instead, she chose to spend her free time tending to the horses on her parents farm and exploring the dozens of trails on the land.

Nina's parents were not farmers. They were scientists who worked in a big, important lab somewhere. She explained to her friends that their jobs were "high stress" and that's why they bought a farm. It was peaceful. And aside from the horses, there were no other animals to care for. And there were no real crops other than a run of the mill vegetable garden.

They were often busy, distracted with one project or another. And Nina was often alone, but she relished the time to herself.

Tim emerged from the waves and reached for her hand.

"The water is great," he coaxed. "Come in with me."

She smiled.

Then she saw them.

Men, dozens of them, were spanning out across the crowded beach each wearing the same style black suit and each with a silver badge pinned to the jacket.

They must be looking for Eva.

Tim noticed, too.

"I really thought she would have shown up by now," he whispered. "I mean she just got mad at her mom or something, right?"

But deep inside he knew something was very wrong. No one ever went missing here before. Briny Deep was safe; everyone knew each other and looked out for each other. It was actually a little creepy how much neighbors seemed to watch each other's comings and goings. At one time, Tim had actually thought they were just watching him. But he quickly realized that would just be silly.

"Why do you think they're looking on the beach?" Nina asked, moving closer to Tim.

He watched the men as they surveyed the shore line.

"I don't know."

Some of the men had rakes and used them to sift through the sand. Another was on his knees picking up something and depositing it in a plastic bag. A few of the men had started to approach people in the crowd, maybe to ask questions? Others were staring into the crowd of beachgoers, but looking for what?

Suddenly, he noticed one man was looking right at him.

Chapter 3

A Few Questions

Quickly averting his eyes, Tim turned to face Nina, but she and Emily had wandered off down by the water. How had they gotten so far away?

"Excuse me, son," said the man, placing his unusually large hand on Tim's shoulder. "I'm an investigator and I'd like to ask you a few questions."

"Uh . . . sure," Tim stammered in reply.

"Do you know the missing girl, Eva?"

"Yeah, everyone knows Eva. I mean . . . we didn't hang out a lot, but we knew each other from school."

The man's pensive eyes bore right through him, and for a moment, Tim wondered if he could read his mind.

After what felt like an eternity, another question.

"Did you notice anyone unfamiliar in town over the past few days?"

"No, no one I don't . . ." Tim's voice trailed off.

The man stared, waiting for the rest of the sentence, but Tim was lost in thought. He actually had seen a stranger several days ago.

"I did see someone I never saw before," he stammered. "I forgot all about it because it seemed like no big deal."

Before he could explain, the man lightly gripped his shoulder, ushering him toward the search area where the rest of the men now gathered.

Two men came forward and stared silently at Tim.

"Tell us exactly what you saw," said the man with big hands.

Tim nervously recalled the encounter.

It was at Luke's house. Luke's mom had died when he was pretty young, and his dad never remarried. With no siblings, the two had become extremely close.

Luke's dad was a great guy.

When Tim was much younger, he had made the mistake of referring to him as Mr. Eller.

"Mr. Eller?" he repeated with mock sarcasm. "That's my dad. Call me Rusty, okay?"

"Sure, Mr. El—I mean Rusty," Tim had laughed.

Rusty's hair was as red as the raspberries he grew in his enormous garden, the one his wife had started years ago.

Luke hadn't inherited the color. His was jet black.

Tim hung out at Luke's house a lot. Luke's dad often traveled out of town on business, and the two of them enjoyed the freedom this allowed.

On the day Tim saw the stranger, Rusty had just gotten back from a trip. He had gone to the outside shed to put away his suitcase. The boys were looking forward to him cooking outside on the grill. The meal would eventually lead to an all-night talk by their huge fire pit.

Their mouths watering and their stomachs burbling, Tim and Luke anxiously waited for him to come back inside so they could get started.

Eventually, Luke had run upstairs to shower, leaving Tim alone.

What was taking Rusty so long?

Tim went to the back door, and just as he was about to take a peek outside, the door swung open and in he came.

"Who's ready for some barbecue?"

"I'm so ready," laughed Tim.

As the door closed slowly behind Luke's dad, Tim spotted the stranger.

Standing on a small hill overlooking Luke's property, he silently stared at the house.

He certainly was not from town. His white blond hair, cropped close to his head, was in stark contrast to the boring way people always styled theirs in Briny Deep.

That was all he remembered. The man had turned and walked away almost immediately. And that was that.

The investigator's questions came popping at him like rain from an unexpected storm, quick and penetrating.

What exactly did the stranger look like?

Did he say anything?

Did he appear threatening?

When it was over, Tim felt dizzy.

He had no information to give. He hadn't seen the guy for more than a few seconds. The only thing that made it odd was the fact that he was a stranger—and strangers just aren't that common in Briny Deep.

The investigator had handed him a card with a phone number, in case he thought of anything else. Tim's stomach hurt.

He made his way back to his friends who riddled him with even more questions.

Nina stood beside him, concerned.

"What did they want?" she asked softly.

"It was no big deal," he replied. "They just asked if I had seen anyone new in town."

Emily moved in closer.

"Have you?" she asked.

Tim told his friends about the man with the short yellow hair.

"Oh, man!" Max nearly shouted. "I've seen him, too."

Tim's throat felt dry.

All eyes settled on Max who seemed to have spontaneously turned two shades whiter.

"He was outside my house last night, sitting on the bench across the street."

"What does it mean?" Emily asked. "Do you think this guy had something to do with Eva being gone?"

Tim shook off the eerie chill that shot down his spine and tried to look calm.

"I'm sure he was just someone visiting a friend for the day," he assured his group. "Gone long before Eva wondered off, and that's all this is. Eva probably just got mad at her parents, like she always does, and is trying to make them feel bad by hiding out somewhere. I bet she's back home by tonight."

Saying the words made Tim feel better.

"Look," he continued. "Let's just all go back to the water and forget about this for a while."

Everyone eagerly agreed.

The rest of the day was spent eating, swimming, and laughing. In fact, they were having so much fun, it was easy to forget that Eva was still gone.

Chapter 4

Party Games

That night, the boys met up at Luke's house. His dad was back in town and had invited everyone over for a last day of summer feasting.

"Hope you guys are hungry," Rusty called out as he balanced several plates of marinated meat and headed out the back door to the grill.

They most certainly were.

The girls would be arriving soon, as well as most of their other friends from school.

All the kids loved Rusty's house.

Actually, 'house' was probably not the right word. It was a huge, rambling estate where one could easily get lost. But not Tim. He knew every nook and cranny of the house and every trail, path, and hill on the land where it sat.

They had all shared a lot of great memories at this place.

As young kids, they spent hours upon hours playing outside—games like tag, hide and seek, or some other crazy made-up game. They had a lot of those.

Some days they could be found climbing the massive trees that dotted the property, and other days they explored the massive spider web of nature trails spanning the grassy acreage.

But truth be told, the best times were had inside.

The massive house smelled of fresh wood. It had three floors as well as an attic and an enormous basement. Its long hallways led to room after room just waiting to be explored.

During one particularly intense game of hide and seek, it had taken his friends over an hour to locate his hiding spot.

There were just so many good places to disappear in this house.

Everyone had started to arrive for the last gathering of summer. In a few days, it would be back to school.

A huge bonfire roared. The flames from dozens of torches staked out across the property rose into the air.

Typically, there would be music from some local live band. But tonight's cookout was a quieter, more somber event because Eva had not come home yet.

"I thought of canceling it," Rusty had said to them earlier. "But I think it's good for everyone to be together, to have a little fun, and get their mind off everything for a night."

Within about an hour, dozens of kids had arrived. Some were eating hot dogs and hamburgers, a few had started up a game of volleyball, and others were milling around talking and catching up with friends.

But everyone had the same thing on their minds—Eva.

It was dark now and a full day had passed since she had gone missing.

"Hey," called out Max as he rode up the path on his skateboard, kicking it up into his hands as he reached Tim. "Want to go get some food?"

Tim nodded in agreement. The two headed down to the massive grill, selected two juicy burgers, and then proceeded to fill the remaining space on their plates with beans, potato salad, and some sort of marshmallow fruit thing.

Luke ran up behind them and grabbed a roll.

"Where are the girls?" he asked.

"Not sure, should be here somewhere," Tim responded, wiping barbecue sauce from his chin.

He needed a napkin; a bit of the sticky sauce still clung to his face. As he turned to grab one from the table, he was face to face with Nina.

"Hey you," she whispered.

How could two little words sound so perfect?

"Hey back," he tried to sound as sultry as she did, but quickly remembered the sauce on his face and felt like a jerk.

"I was looking for you . . ." he continued, but noticing Emily standing there, too, changed his wording mid-speak.

"I was looking for you girls."

Nina smiled and gazed up at him with those eyes, those perfectly green eyes.

"I made cookies," she teased. "You have to try them."

She didn't have to ask twice.

Tim felt light-headed. Or maybe it was just love.

It started when they were young kids. Their parents had shipped them off to a sleep-away camp just beyond the mountains north and to the west of Briny Deep. It was a week in the woods: fishing, hiking, swimming in the lake, and telling stories by the bonfire. It was by the light of one of those bonfires that he saw her eyes for the first time—really saw them—and how impossibly green and beautiful they were.

Underneath the starry sky, they had shared their dreams of the future. He aspired to be a doctor, and her a scientist like her parents. They had laughed and talked for hours, brushing each other's hands as they spoke. She had gently pushed his shoulder and tugged his sleeve when he would say something particularly funny.

Since that night, their relationship had changed. There was a tender undercurrent of attraction. But through the years that followed, and as they got older, he had been unable to express to her what he felt. Every day that he remained silent made it tougher and more impossible to ever approach the subject with her. He was sure he would carry this agony to his grave.

"Let's play hide and seek!" someone yelled from across the yard, rousing Tim from the fog his mind had suddenly gotten lost in.

"Inside!" called Luke pointing a long finger toward the imposing house.

About ten of them ran inside . . . and the game began.

Chapter 5

Hide and Seek

They hadn't played for a long time. Not inside.

Everyone scurried off in a different direction. Luke was "it" and he began the countdown.

"1 . . . 2 . . . 3 . . . 4 . . ."

Tim took to the stairs and ascended quickly to the third floor. He spotted Emily running into a room down the hall and a brief glimpse of Nina's foot as she climbed the last set of stairs leading to the attic.

. . . Nina . . .

No time for that now, he thought, and ran to the end of the hall. He turned the corner and sprinted up the second hallway to an area that was rarely visited. It was used mostly to store big pieces of furniture and other knickknacks Rusty had collected in his travels.

Large armoires; oversized canopied beds; huge, exotic looking trunks and wardrobes— there were just so many places to hide.

It had been awhile since he was last here. Tim wandered down the vast hallway, peering into the rooms with open doors as he passed. He walked slowly, almost forgetting he was in the middle of a game.

It was just so odd to be here again.

From somewhere far away, he barely heard Luke's call.

"Ready or not, here I come!"

Tim picked up the pace.

As he neared the end of the hallway, he noticed something he hadn't before.

A door . . .

. . . and it was closed.

Curious, he put his hand on the knob and turned. It was locked.

Strange.

He looked up at the wall to the right of the door. A framed photograph hung there. It was of two small children—two boys.

It was grainy and faded. Tim squinted and tried to make out the other two people beside the boys in the image.

Wait . . . isn't that . . . Rusty?

Yeah, it was Rusty . . . and his wife Lenore. They were much younger in this photo, but Tim was sure now that it was them.

He looked closely at the two boys.

With an unmistakable black mop of hair, one was clearly Luke, but who was the other?

Footsteps . . . he heard footsteps . . . Luke.

Tim spun around, retraced his steps up the hallway, and slipped into a familiar room. He climbed into the giant wardrobe and quietly closed the door, leaving it open just a hair so he could hear if Luke approached. He certainly did not want to be the first one found. He had a reputation and a record to uphold.

After what had to be thirty minutes, Tim's foot was asleep and his back hurt from crouching over.

This was not as much fun as he remembered.

He cracked open the door a bit and peered out . . . no one there.

Tim climbed out of the wardrobe—he couldn't breathe in there anymore—too musty.

"Gotcha!" Luke screamed at the top of his lungs.

Tim shrieked in surprise.

After the shock wore off, neither could stop laughing for several minutes.

"Last to be found again, huh?" Tim chortled. "I'm still the reigning hide and seek champ."

Luke eyed him up and down.

"Sorry, champ, but there's another. I haven't been able to find Anthony yet."

Tim frowned.

"Ugh, my record is broken by Anthony? The kid already wins like every award in school."

Luke laughed, and the two headed down to the bottom landing where Max and Nina were waiting. Luke continued on alone down another flight of stairs to the basement where he was sure Anthony must be held up.

Everyone else headed back outside.

Nina grabbed Tim by the hand and led him away from the group.

"Walk?" she suggested. "It's such a beautiful night."

He felt light-headed again.

The couple strolled along a path, past friends playing Frisbee and others running around trying to tag each other.

"So, are you looking forward to school starting up?" she asked jokingly because she already knew the answer. No one looks forward to school after a great summer break like they had just experienced.

"Uh, sure," he laughed.

Nina looked serious now. She leaned close to Tim's ear, "What do you really think happened to Eva?"

He stopped and turned to face her, taking both her hands in his. If he answered wrong, he knew he would just upset her.

"She'll come back. In fact, I bet she's already back home, apologizing up and down to her parents for making them worry so much."

Nina stared into his eyes.

"I don't think so, Tim."

He had never seen her like this before. She was really scared.

The flames from a nearby torch blazed behind her in the distance, illuminating her hair, giving her an angelic glow. It reminded him of the first time he ever noticed her at summer camp—really noticed her.

She leaned in closer, and the next thing Tim knew she was clinging to him.

He hugged her back.

"Nina," he said softly. "Everything will be okay."

That's when they heard it.

Several voices were calling out.

"Anthony?"

"Anthony!"

The panic was evident.

Nina and Tim released their grip on each other and ran toward the commotion.

"Can't find Anthony anywhere," Luke said breathlessly. "He's just gone."

Chapter 6

Vanished

The little girl kicks the ball. Tim chases after it, but the bright yellow orb goes flying under a table in the back part of the playground.

Laughing.

The voices of children everywhere.

A tall, leafy tree hangs low over the table, obscuring it from sight.

Tim is on his knees now, crawling under the table, extending his hand toward the ball. But it's just out of reach.

Creeping further into the darkness, he feels the fabric on his pants tear away at the knee.

But he will not be deterred.

Further under the table he goes, stretching his arm until he can feel the smooth surface of the ball.

He grasps it with his fingertips, pulling it toward him.

As he begins to inch his way back out, he is startled by a noise.

Did someone just scream out for help?

The man pursuing him is close; he can hear twigs snap under heavy feet, pounding into the grass just behind him. Ahead, a patch of flowers and a yellow house, if he can just get there . . .

Tim's eyes pop open as he quickly sits straight up in bed, covered in sweat, his heart racing.

It was the same nightmare with the same yellow house . . . but not exactly the same.

This time there was a bit more.

The ball, some girl, and a scream?

"Ugh, whatever," he sighed with disgust.

He felt as though he hadn't slept at all. It was the first day back at school, and for the first time he could remember, Tim was not looking forward to it at all.

Eva was still missing.

And now Anthony was gone, too.

What was happening?

At the party two nights ago, they had searched everywhere. But Anthony was nowhere to be found.

He wasn't home. He wasn't anywhere.

The police had been called and arrived on the scene within minutes.

They searched, they questioned everyone. Anthony was gone.

Once the sun had come out, the grounds were searched again, but to no avail. And another night passed with no answers and no sign of Eva or Anthony.

Tim dragged himself out of bed and headed into the bathroom for a shower.

He let the hot water wash over him. This was going to be a long day.

After a quick change into khakis and a white shirt, he leaped down the stairs two at a time. He blew past the kitchen where his mother was making breakfast.

"Tim?" she called to him. "Eat something."

He breezed past her, planting a small kiss on her cheek, before hightailing it out the front door.

"Not hungry, Mom. See you later."

"Tim, be careful!" she called out just before he hopped on his skateboard and headed down the winding road to school.

The school was a large, two-story brick building with stairs leading to a massive entryway. But he was early—not time to go inside yet. So he headed to the common area out front and sat along the edge of the fountain, a meeting spot for students.

He put his backpack down and surveyed the crowd. There seemed to be even more people than usual milling about.

Oh, and Nina was here already, several dozen feet away, her back turned to him. She was talking to some guy.

Who was that?

He couldn't quite make him out.

Tim craned his neck a bit to see . . .

"Hey, bro."

Luke had sidled up right beside him and he hadn't even noticed.

Tim turned to him and laughed.

"Geez, man, you're like a phantom."

Luke chuckled back, but his eyes took on a serious note as he looked around.

"Do you see them?" he asked.

"See who?"

Luke turned back to his friend.

"The men," he whispered. "The police, I guess. They're everywhere."

Tim looked again.

How had he not noticed them before?

He suspected it was probably because he had only been interested in what Nina was doing and with whom she was talking at the moment.

There must have been at least ten of them, talking to students and teachers. Two of them were stationed right by the school's entrance just observing the crowd.

Max motioned a greeting from across the lawn and jogged up to his friends.

"I think someone else is missing."

Tim and Luke looked up at him in disbelief.

"You mean Anthony, right?"

"No, man," Max replied softly. "I don't."

The boys stared at each other in silence for a moment.

Tim was afraid to ask, but of course he had to know.

"Who?"

Max lowered his face.

"It's Emily's sister. It's Isabelle."

Tim's throat tightened. He tried to respond, but it took everything he had just to breathe.

The school bell rang out, signaling there were seven minutes left to get to class.

The day went by in a blur. The only part he really remembered was the morning announcement that curfew was now in effect; no one allowed out after dark.

Emily was not in school that day or the next.

On the third day, she came back, her eyes red and swollen.

They had all promised to be there for her, whatever she needed.

At lunch, they all sat at the same round table they always did. Emily's food went untouched, and she rested her head on Nina's shoulder.

"Who could have taken Isabelle?" she said through tears.

"Isabelle will be fine," was all Luke could think to say.

"They'll find her," Max added. "I know they will."

Tim was at a complete loss for words.

He had no idea what to say—or what to think. So he just put his hand on Emily's shoulder and squeezed.

Later that night, he sat out on his front porch swing, the front door wide open so his parents could see him at all times per their request.

Who could be doing this? He thought hard. He knew everyone so well. It had to be an outsider.

Then he thought about the stranger he'd seen, the man with the short, yellow hair, standing outside of Luke's house.

But now that he pondered the question for a few moments, he had to admit there were a few "weirdos" in town—people he knew less than others.

Like the strange woman who always stared out her window and hardly ever came outside. Or Mr. Kull, who yelled at any kid who tried to cut through his yard, a shortcut to the beach.

But why?

Why would anyone be taking the kids of Briny Deep?

Tim was so lost in thought, he hadn't seen Luke approaching the house until he was standing right in front of him. He had clearly been running and was visibly shaken.

"Luke, what the . . . ?"

"That stranger . . . ," Luke gasped, trying to catch his breath. "The one we both saw."

"Yeah? What about him?"

"He's after me!"

Chapter 7

Followed

Luke rushed past Tim and hurried inside the house.

"Come on! He's out there!"

Tim jumped up and took a long look into the darkness.

Nothing moved. It was silent. And then . . . he saw something, just behind a tree, a shadow.

Yellow hair.

Tim was so startled he nearly knocked a planter over in his hurry to get inside.

Both boys ran until they were at the top of the stairs.

"What's going on?" Tim's mom called out.

"Mom, he's out there, the stranger I told the police about!"

"He followed . . ."

Before the words had left his mouth, Tim's dad had grabbed a bat and was outside.

After running up and down the street a few times, it was clear whoever had been out there was now gone.

He came racing back inside.

"Call the police."

When the authorities arrived, they spent over an hour searching the area and questioning Luke about the incident. But whoever had been out there was definitely long gone now.

"I left my house later than I meant to," he explained to his interrogator. "My dad told me to get here before dark, and I guess I just lost track of time."

Because Rusty had been called out of town on some last-minute business, arrangements had been made earlier that morning for Luke to spend the night at Tim's.

"I heard a noise behind me—footsteps—so I turned around and no one was there, but then I saw it."

"You saw what exactly?" asked the officer with just a hint of impatience.

"A man with yellow hair," he said, his voice shaking. "He was just standing behind a tree . . . watching me."

"Did he threaten you or say anything to you?"

"I didn't hang around to find out if he would. I just ran."

After the police left, Tim and Luke retreated to the bedroom, but sleep wasn't easy to come by. So they whispered in the darkness about all the strange events going on in Briny Deep.

At some point, Tim remembered a question he'd been meaning to ask Luke all day. With all the excitement, it had slipped his mind.

"Hey, bro, the other night when we were playing hide and seek in your house, I found a photo of your parents . . . with another kid. Who is that?"

Luke turned pale.

"You found a photo of him?" he whispered. "I thought they had gotten rid of all the photos."

Tim stared at his friend, not wanting to push too much. This was clearly not a good memory for him.

"That was my brother," Luke said, his head hanging down. "He died when I was still pretty young, just before my mom."

Tim's eyes opened wide with amazement.

How did he not know this?

Why had no one ever mentioned it?

He sensed that Luke was getting upset. And with all the drama he'd already suffered earlier, Tim figured it was best to change the topic. But he did make a mental note to talk to him more about it later, once everything else had calmed down.

By three o'clock in the morning, the boys had exhausted themselves talking about the man with the yellow hair, the missing kids, and the people they thought were strange in town.

The next day, school whizzed by. Armed security guards were situated at every entry and exit. All everyone talked about were the missing kids. Some kids weren't in school because their parents had decided it was too dangerous to let them out of their sight, so there were a lot less bodies walking the halls.

After school, Luke headed back home to pick up another change of clothes because his dad had been detained out of town another night. Tim and Max had offered to go with him, but in the light of day, any kind of fear Luke had about the stranger was gone. So instead, the two boys made a stop at Emily's house to check on her. Nina was already there, trying very hard to offer her some comfort.

The mood in the house was solemn. Tim and Max each took a seat but weren't sure what to say.

"I heard you saw him," a stern voice called from the stairs.

It was Emily's dad.

He was a big, imposing man. Not one for small talk and certainly not the kind to be crossed, thought Tim.

"The stranger, you saw him . . . and Luke . . . Luke saw him, too," he continued, sounding almost accusatory. "Well, am I right?"

Now he sounded angry.

"Only for a minute, sir," Tim said softly. "And I think the same guy followed Luke the other night."

From somewhere behind Emily's dad, another voice joined in the conversation.

"We have no indication there was ever a stranger," said a cold, harsh voice.

The man who had just spoken appeared from the shadows and approached Tim.

"Young man, you and your friend Luke are the only people who claim to have seen this stranger with the yellow hair."

As he spoke, the man used two fingers to put air quotes around the word "seen."

"No one else in town has seen him, why do you think that is?"

Tim shrugged and looked down at his feet.

"Eva's parents said she had seen him, too," he said.

This man looked hard at Tim and shook his head.

"We think it was likely someone else— someone she knew."

It was then that Tim noticed the badge. He was with the police; one of the same guys that had been on the beach a few days ago.

"You mean someone from town?" Tim stammered.

"Yes," he answered. "Maybe even someone you know."

"Someone I know?"

After eyeing Tim for a few more moments, the officer turned to Emily's father and the two disappeared into the den together.

Following a bit more small talk with his friends, Tim said an awkward good-bye to the group and made the short walk up the street to his house, looking nervously behind him only once . . . maybe twice.

Chapter 8

Where Is Luke?

When he reached the steps of his house, Tim noticed that Luke's bike wasn't out front. He'd made a big deal out of telling his dad on the phone that he would ride his bike over right after he grabbed an outfit from home. Since it wasn't there that meant neither was Luke.

Tim grabbed the skateboard he'd left upside down in the front yard and headed down the hill to Luke's house. Dusk was falling and even though the sun was still up, it wouldn't be for long. It made him chuckle a little to imagine Luke's face once he realized he lost track of time again and it was getting dark.

Besides, he couldn't wait to tell Luke about the angry guy and his insinuation that they simply hadn't seen what they claimed. Like he thought they imagined it, or worse, made it up.

He glided down the path leading to Luke's front door. When he got to the end, he jumped off the board and jogged up the front steps.

Tim knocked—once, twice.

No answer.

He peered in the window. Nothing moved.

He reached for the door and turned the knob. The door creaked open, and Tim walked inside.

The house was silent. He walked in a little farther and called out.

"Luke?"

No response.

He started to head across the house to the stairs but stopped before reaching them.

Something felt weird . . . almost like he was being watched. He didn't like it.

For a moment he was frozen in the same spot, unsure whether to move forward or go back.

He listened for any sound—almost afraid to hear one.

Why did he feel so uneasy? This was practically his second home.

He was just being silly. Luke was probably waiting for him at his house right now.

He turned and walked quickly toward the front door. In his mind, he envisioned a hand falling hard on his shoulder, grabbing him back into the house.

It seemed to take twice as long to make his way back. When he finally reached the door, he was moving so fast that his heart was pounding and his breathing was labored. But he didn't take even a second to catch his breath.

He hopped right on his board and headed home.

As he approached his house, he noticed his mom was outside. The sun was just about to set. It would be dark within minutes.

"Where is Luke?" she asked when he was closer.

Tim suddenly felt very cold.

"He's not here?"

She slowly shook her head and her eyes grew wide.

≈ ≈ ≈ ≈ ≈

The man pursuing him is close; he can hear twigs snap under heavy feet, pounding into the grass just behind him. Ahead, a patch of flowers and a yellow house, if he can just get there, but then he remembers he won't make it.

He never does.

The rock, hidden in the grass, is steps away. Tim trips, landing on his knees, a strong hand grips his shoulder, pulling him away again.

When Tim opened his eyes, he was covered in sweat.

His heart was racing as it usually did after the nightmare. As the fog of sleep faded away and he became more alert to the sun shining in his face, a sharp pain ripped through his stomach, as the painful memory that sleep had subdued came back full force.

Four kids were missing: Eva, Anthony, Isabelle, and now Luke.

In the days following Luke's disappearance, the town of Briny Deep was thrown into an all-out state of emergency.

As far as anyone in town knew, there was no sign of any of them. They had simply— vanished.

It had been decided that schools would be closed, in addition to every road in and out of Briny Deep.

Curfew had been extended to all day. With the exception of adults going to work and getting supplies like food, gas, and other necessities, no one was allowed off their own property.

Children were to stay indoors at all times. No exceptions. At least one adult was required to remain home in order to watch over the kids and make sure this rule was followed without fail.

Tim groaned in pain, though not the physical kind. He sat up, threw his legs over the side of his bed, and hunched over with his elbows on his knees and his hands covering his eyes. He was so caught up in a mix of anguish and confusion that he hadn't heard his mother enter the room. She sat down next to him and extended an arm around her son's back.

"I'm just so glad that you are safe," she said softly in his ear.

It was of no comfort to Tim.

Something was *very wrong* in Briny Deep and he was going to find out what.

If the authorities couldn't find his friends— then *he* would.

Chapter 9

Strangers Among Us

The four met in secrecy.

They had to be so careful now. The town was crawling with authorities.

It had been a highly successful trip, but there was one more thing they needed to do, one more thing that *must be done* before they returned home.

Home . . . ?

The man with the yellow hair thought about the word for a while.

He was ready to go home. But his job was not yet complete. *Their* job was not complete.

He looked around the room at his partners; a motley crew of mercenaries. Like most in their profession, instead of using real names, they each had a nickname.

First, there was "Lone Star," who chose hers for being born and bred in Texas. Then "Blaze" for his red hair. Another called himself "Mud Puppy," a name earned in the Army. And finally there was "Canary," for his blond hair.

Under the circumstances, the names were too long to actually use, so they went by the initials L. S., B., M. P., and C.

The house where they stayed was off the grid.

Way off.

No one would suspect where it was, or even bother looking in the area. It was a perfect hideout. Hidden in the forest, and bathed in large, old trees, the outside of the large two-story wood cabin blended in flawlessly with its surroundings.

But he was anxious to get this whole thing over with. He was ready to move on.

"Okay, let's get started," Canary called to the group. "We all know what the objective is now, but the question is how do we achieve it? The town is on complete lockdown."

It's not as if they hadn't anticipated this. They had. A major reaction is appropriate when four kids go missing.

But what they didn't count on was a group of kids who didn't follow the rules. *They* were definitely becoming a problem. Moving around unseen was getting increasingly difficult, and they were not ready to leave . . . not yet.

"We just continue with the plan and we don't deviate from it," M. P. cautioned.

L. S. stood up from a large leather chair and walked right up to him, getting close enough to look him right in the eyes.

"I say leave with what you got now," she snarled. "Those kids are nothing but trouble, and if you stick around, you'll find that out."

"We are under strict orders," B. fired back. "You know that."

L. S. grunted and turned her back to him and faced Canary.

"You know what could happen," she said. "Do you really want to risk it?"

Canary knew exactly what could happen, but he had no choice. They had to see this mission through to the end. No matter what the risk.

Taking Eva had been almost too easy.

She constantly bickered with her parents and made a habit of storming out of the house. Her favorite place to go and cool off from an argument was the forest—she practically delivered herself right to their front doorstep. Eva hadn't been scared at first. Certainly she never thought someone would try and kidnap her. Not in this safe haven where crime of any kind was practically a nonissue. But once she realized what was happening, she had cried and called out for help. But there was no one to hear her.

Likewise, Anthony had been a relative walk in the park to take.

B. had handled that one. He moved among them with ease. No one thought anything was out of order until it was too late. A game of hide and seek was the ideal moment to nab him. And it didn't hurt that Anthony knew and trusted B. He fell right into the trap.

Isabelle was a little trickier. Being younger and under the watchful eye of her overbearing, militant parents had made finding the right moment to take her difficult.

L. S. had played that one perfectly, being a female. What little girl would think she was one of the "kidnappers?" Usually brutish and hard, L. S. managed to find her softer side long enough to convince Isabelle to help her find a lost puppy, which of course she happily agreed to do. Yeah, Isabelle never suspected a thing.

Certainly, the most difficult acquisition was Luke.

He was already big for his age, standing nearly six feet tall, athletic, and muscular. They knew he was not going to be easy. Especially when B.

had to attend to other important business on the same night they planned to take him.

And then there was the fact that Canary had been careless. Outside of Luke's house, both Luke and Tim had seen him. But it wasn't a problem because no one believed them. Canary had made sure of that.

They had seen him again outside Tim's house. So when Canary finally did come face to face with Luke, you can bet he was terrified. Come to think of it, he had screamed, but it didn't matter because no one could hear anything that went on inside that big house of his.

They were home free with one exception.

Tim.

He was the last one they needed.

Chapter 10

A Time for Heroes

The four met in secrecy.

They had to be so careful now. The town was crawling with authorities.

Tim, Nina, Max, and Emily were going against everything their parents and the police had told them to do. Kids were not allowed off their own property. The town was shut down like a clogged drain—nothing getting in or out—except perhaps four clever kids.

Tim had told his mom that he was going to sleep early. His parents bought it because he'd been so depressed lately. All he'd been doing was lying in bed, except he hadn't been asleep.

He'd been thinking and planning and plotting a way to find his friends.

He realized that if the authorities really thought he and Luke had made up the story about the stranger that meant the police were not looking for him. So Tim had to find him, before it was too late.

Since they couldn't see each other in person over the last few days, Tim and his friends had been burning up the phone lines to stay in touch. They decided to formulate a plan to rescue their friends.

Max had snuck over a couple times to strategize in person. But when his mom realized he had left, she threw such a fit that both Tim and Max would have certainly been grounded for a month, had they not already been relegated to their house 24/7.

But on this night, the four of them made the same excuse of being tired and headed to their bedrooms, then right out their windows.

Tim and Max met up at a local park and then rode their boards over to get Emily and then

Nina. They didn't want the girls out on their own.

Leaving the skateboards hidden in a bush outside Nina's house, the group silently jogged through the back paths and across the shortcuts in Briny Deep. They stayed off the main roads and away from the watchful eye of authorities.

They made their way behind the school and down the hill to Luke's house.

Once there, Tim was able to open a window in the back by the kitchen. They always left this window unlocked because both Rusty and Luke said the lock was too hard to turn. And anyway, Rusty had reasoned, *'Why bother, who's going to break in?'*

Tim motioned for them to follow him. They stumbled in the dark as they made their way to a large, cozy den just off the main dining room.

He chose this room because it had no windows, so no one would see the small light that went on as he flicked a switch.

They knew the house would be empty because Rusty was at Emily's house right now, getting ready to have a meeting with the police. It would be hours before he returned.

Everyone quickly found a seat.

Tim and Max had to fill the girls in on their plan. It was too dangerous to talk about it over the phone or within earshot of their parents, which is exactly why they had insisted on meeting in person.

Tim explained that the plan they had devised was based on something Max had learned when he was over at Emily's house several days ago. He overheard the grumpy investigator tell Emily's dad that the authorities were staking out a house, Mr. Kull's house, the reclusive man who always yelled at kids when they tried to cut though his yard. The investigator had shared something else, too. They were waiting for him to return because Mr. Kull wasn't there and no one could locate him.

Except maybe for Max . . . Max knew something most people did not. Mr. Kull had done handyman work for Rusty. With such a vast piece of property, there was a lot of work to do, and Rusty didn't have the time or the desire to do it.

At this point, Max took over the story.

He explained to the girls that more than a year ago, he and Luke had been climbing trees on Luke's land. It used to be one of their favorite ways to spend a lazy afternoon. On this particular day, they had separated in order to find some new spots to climb.

Max had wandered off deeper into the woods than he'd ever been before.

That was when he came across Mr. Kull.

He was out there, just past a thick band of trees that made him hardly visible, putting the finishing touches on a huge cabin. The construction materials covering the forest floor around him made it clear that this cabin was freshly constructed. And it looked to him like Mr. Kull had done an amazing job.

"I remember thinking at the time, man, Luke is so lucky. Not only does he have the best house in town, and the best land, but now he has this awesome cabin, too."

Max admitted that he wanted to get a closer look. But because Mr. Kull had done his fair share of yelling in Max's direction over the years, he was in no rush to be seen by him and forced into an awkward "Hello." He made his way out of the woods and headed back to find Luke. It was a task that took more than hour, by which time Max had completely put the whole Mr. Kull scenario out of his mind and never mentioned it to Luke. He had actually forgotten about it—until now.

"Okay, here's what we're going to do," Tim began. "We're going to find that cabin because I think that's where they've got our friends."

Nina looked visibly shaken.

"No, Tim, you can't do that!" she practically yelled. "It's way too dangerous. We have to tell our parents."

Her reaction took Tim by surprise. Nina was always the adventurous one—up for anything. She had more courage than anyone he ever knew. He'd never known her to be afraid of anything.

Wait, was she shaking?

"You're right, it might be dangerous, that's why you and Emily aren't coming along," he said looking directly into her eyes . . . her green eyes. "But Max and I are going out tonight to find this cabin and bring our friends home."

Chapter 11

Cabin Fever

Nina was in a panic.

Tim and Max had just explained their plan to her, and even though she begged them not to go through with it, she could see they would not be deterred.

After quickly escorting both girls back to the safety of their respective homes, the boys set off on their own, into the dark maze of woods on Luke's property.

Nina climbed up the trellis leading to her bedroom window and pulled herself inside.

She had to tell someone . . . fast.

≈ ≈ ≈ ≈ ≈

The section of property closest to the house was manicured to the hilt, dotted with flowers, gardens, a huge barbecue pit, and a pond filled with colorful fish. Paths led out to various other areas, including a sand volleyball court, and benches where one could sit and take in all the beauty of nature.

But the path Tim and Max took was not well traveled. It led to the woods and some of the most enormous trees Tim had ever seen.

"I can't remember exactly where it is," said Max. "I found it by accident last time."

So the two boys walked . . . and walked . . . and walked . . .

And the woods became thicker, and darker, and wilder.

Finally, Max stopped.

"This looks like the area."

Tim had no idea how he could tell one area from the next out here, especially in the dark of night.

"Take a good look around," Max whispered. "It's really hard to spot. It's hidden by the trees."

Tim could barely see the ground beneath him. The darkness was overwhelming.

He slowly turned in a circle and tried to make out the shapes around him.

All of them were trees.

There were huge, hovering, massive trees everywhere.

Wait . . . what's that?

Tim squinted, thinking for some crazy reason this would help him see better in the dark.

There . . . just up that hill, was it a . . . ?

"Over there!" Max shouted, immediately realizing that shouting wasn't a smart thing to do right now.

He was pointing at the exact spot Tim had been trying to focus on. It did look like there was something up there—something big.

It was the cabin . . . and there was a light on inside.

~~~~~

Canary was watching, just as he had almost every night for days.

He knew the family would be asleep any minute now. The lights had gone off, as they did each night at ten o'clock on the dot. No earlier and no later—right on schedule. He would give it an hour for everyone to be fast asleep, and then he'd go in the house and get Tim, right from his bed. He wouldn't know what was happening until it was done.

~~~~~

Nina paced the length of her room. Her parents were in a closed-door meeting over at Emily's house, and every attempt to reach them had failed. She *must* get through, even if it meant walking over there herself.

~~~~~

Tim and Max tried their best to walk silently, but with every step, twigs would snap and leaves crunched under their feet. Tim winced when he stepped right on a pine comb that seemed to explode with sound.

They made their way through the thick wooded brush and up the hill leading to the cabin.

As they got closer, they could see that the light inside was flickering—maybe it was a candle?

Max reached the cabin first and waited for Tim to catch up. Once he did, they crouched down and quietly discussed their next move. They needed to get closer to see if anyone was inside. But nerves were getting the best of them right now.

Tim stood up.

"Okay, let's go."

The boys walked to the back of the cabin and up to a small window. Max peered inside.

"I can't see anything."

Tim motioned Max towards a larger window. They kneeled down and crawled under it, waiting just a moment for a burst of courage before they stood up to look in.

Finally it came. They rose up together and looked inside.

They could see the candle flickering on a table just a few feet away. It illuminated a large room that was empty for the most part, except for what looked like a leather couch, a chair, and a large table with several chairs around it.

There was no sign of anybody inside . . . yet.

The boys moved farther down to another window and peered in—it was a kitchen. A few coffee cups littered the countertop, and a plate with the remnants of some meal lay in the sink. But there was no sign of any people.

"Let's see if one of these windows is open," Tim whispered.

Chapter 12

Secret Revealed

It's weird, Canary thought as he silently lifted up the window to Tim's bedroom and slipped stealthily inside. No one ever locks their windows in this town.

As his eyes adjusted to the darkness, he realized that Tim was gone. For the very first time, a stab of panic gripped him, but just for a moment.

He was out the window and racing down the road toward Luke and Rusty's property within seconds . . .

≈ ≈ ≈ ≈ ≈

Tim could not believe they were actually inside the cabin. He and Max had tried every window and even the front door, but everything was locked. This was except for one unlatched window just off the kitchen that was just large enough for them both to climb through.

There was just one large room downstairs with a bathroom and the kitchen off to the side. A small spiral staircase led upstairs to what appeared to be a loft.

They moved closer to the table. Papers were scattered across it. Tim picked one up.

It was a map of some sort, unlike any he'd ever seen before. He had no idea where any of the places on it were.

He put it down and grabbed another paper. It was in some sort of code. He couldn't make it out.

He reached for another paper. It read:

1. Eva
2. Anthony
3. Isabelle
4. Luke

It was a list and the last name on it was very familiar:

5. Tim

He looked at Max, who was already staring right back at him.

"We found their hideout."

Realizing that his friends could be held somewhere in this cabin and acutely aware that the kidnapper could come back at any moment, Tim quickly ascended the steps two-at-a-time to the loft. It was empty except for a small nightstand with one drawer and a well-worn mattress on the ground.

He eyed the nightstand as Max came up the steps.

"You should have waited for me, bro," he said in a winded voice. "I found some photos."

"Max, my name was on the list!" Tim cried out.

"What list?"

"It's a list of all the kids who have disappeared and me."

Max dropped the pictures he was holding.

"Could one of those detectives be staying here?"

"Why would my name be on it?" Tim called out as he headed for the nightstand. He looked down at the tiny handle that opened the drawer and pulled. There were just two items inside.

Tim pulled out the first. It was a small necklace.

Best Friends Forever

It was Isabelle's.

He peered into the drawer to see what the other item was. It was a woven bracelet—a perfect match to his.

He turned back to Max.

"Let's see if there's a basement."

~~~~~

Once back on the property, and being an expert at tracking, it was easy for Canary to deduce that the two sets of footprints he had found led right to the cabin.

He battled through the brush and branches, reaching the outside of the cabin within minutes where he nimbly climbed a very tall tree to get a better view inside. Canary could see the boys clearly now. They were running around inside the cabin. It was obvious they had seen something that had really scared them.

They came right to me, Canary chuckled.

This is going to be easier than I thought.

~ ~ ~ ~ ~

There was no basement. But there was a room they hadn't noticed before. The door was closed. Max pushed it open slowly and they both walked inside.

It was too dark to see a thing. Then a light went on. The man with yellow hair was waiting.

"Hello, boys."

~ ~ ~ ~ ~

Nina ran as fast as she could, but it still seemed to take an eternity to reach Emily's house. Once there, she burst in the front door. Inside, the room was full. Her parents, Emily's parents, and several others were in the middle of a conversation. They all turned toward her in surprise.

"It's Tim and Max," she cried. "They're in danger!"

~ ~ ~ ~ ~

They were in a lot of trouble.

The man with the yellow hair had injected something into their arms and Tim could feel himself getting dizzy. Now he was leading them back to the loft.

"Please sit down," as he motioned to the mattress.

Too late, thought Tim.

It was his last thought before he fell, unconscious, onto the mattress next to Max. Canary grabbed his phone and dialed the number.

"We got him," he told the person on the other end. "Got another one, too, they're both ready for transport—immediately."

He kept one eye on the boys as he listened intently to the voice on the phone.

"This was unavoidable," he responded firmly. "Yes, I understand and I . . . wait, hold a moment."

Canary stood silent.

He heard something outside.

"Abort!" he yelled into the phone. "Abort!"

Tim lifted his head. He was so groggy.

Canary dropped the phone as he heard the front door kicked open and glass shattering in the back part of the cabin.

Seeing the photos on the floor beneath him, he dropped to his knees and sifted through them haphazardly trying to find it . . . the one of the . . . where was it?

Tim was sitting straight up now, staring at him. Canary crawled over to him, as feet pounded up the stairs toward him.

"Tim!" he called out. "Look at this, please."

Tim looked groggily over at his friend Max who was still asleep, and then back at the man with the yellow hair.

"Look . . . at what?" he said as he almost lost consciousness again. He was so dizzy.

Canary handed him a photo and Tim tried to focus on it. It was a yellow house, the same yellow house from his dreams.

"This is your house," the man with yellow hair said. "This is your home . . . on Earth."

"I came here to rescue you . . . to take you home!"

Suddenly, men with badges were everywhere. They had the stranger down on the ground and handcuffed. Then they dragged him to his feet and down the stairs.

He was able to see that two of the men were running over to him just before he drifted back into darkness.

≈ ≈ ≈ ≈ ≈

"Hey."

The soft, sweet voice called to him.

"Tim, I'm here and you're safe."

He opened his eyes slowly and with much effort. They felt heavy as lead.

Nina was there with him.

She was holding his hand, smiling.

He was in a hospital bed, machines beeped around him. His parents were there, too.

"We are so relieved," his mom said taking his other hand.

His dad nodded and winked.

"You're going to be just fine, son," he said.

"What about Max?" Tim managed to ask.

"He's doing very good," his dad answered. "He's already awake and walking around."

A man with a badge, approached the bed.

"You're a very lucky young man. We have the kidnapper in custody," he said looking intently at Tim. "But we didn't find the other kids, only some of their belongings. Did you see the others?"

"No," Tim replied sadly.

"Okay, we're going to let you rest," said the investigator as he turned to the door. "When you feel better, we'll talk some more."

Then he was gone.

His mother looked at him and then took his dad's arm, leading him out the door as well.

"Yes, I think rest is exactly what you need," she said. "Get some sleep."

Only Nina stayed behind.

"I had to tell them about your plan, Tim. I was so afraid for you."

Tim looked into her eyes.

"I'm really glad you did," he managed a small laugh.

He was relieved that he and Max were alive and here, safe, with family and friends.

But his heart ached for the others. There was no way he would ever give up trying to find the missing kids—his friends.

Then he remembered. Something he had forgotten. Something the man with the yellow hair had said—the yellow house . . . his house?

"Nina," he whispered. "Where is Earth?"

Read the Chapter 1 teaser from *The Return* . . .

Back to the Beginning

It was a normal day.

The sun was big and bright within a blue sky that was filled with puffy white clouds.

Laughter filled the air as children amused themselves outside the small nursery school. A young girl giggled with delight as the ball she threw bopped a little boy right on his head. Another squealed with joy as his tiny plastic car sailed down a long toy ramp.

As the young teacher kept careful watch over her students, she could see the playground alive with activity—every swing taken and a sandbox full of happy faces.

Ms. Wolpert loved her job at the school. She had gotten it right out of college and considered herself blessed to have a career around children. She loved each and every one of them—and they loved her right back.

"Here, Ms. Wolpert, I made this for you," said a little girl with big eyes and blonde pigtails.

The teacher took the work of art and carefully studied the picture of a tall woman with dark hair, long eyelashes, and red lips which she could see must be her. Holding her hand was a little girl with golden pigtails—and the word love written in big crayon letters above.

"Oh, Polly, this is a masterpiece," she cooed as she ran her hand atop Polly's head. "I absolutely love it."

Polly grinned widely and stood up on her tippy toes to whisper in her teacher's ear.

"You can take it home with you if you want to."

"I do Polly, I really do! Thank you!"

She knew she wasn't supposed to have favorites—and she didn't. But she hoped that one day she would have a little girl just like Polly.

With her mission accomplished, Polly ran back to join the other kids.

"Another love note?" said Ms. Horne with a smile. "You have become quite popular in your first year here."

Ms. Horne, who had been at the school for nearly ten years, was a trusted mentor to the young teacher and also a dear friend.

"I'm going to run inside and try to grade a few papers. Think you can handle things out here on your own?" she asked.

"Of course, you go ahead," Ms. Wolpert replied.

"Thank you so much, and listen, do me a favor, keep an eye on Matthew. He still seems a bit shy around the other kids, and I worry that he's spending too much time alone."

"Yes, I noticed that, too. I'll check on him now," said Ms. Wolpert as her eyes scouted the playground for little Matthew.

Just then a shadow passed over the school darkening the yard for a moment. She looked up to see if the beautiful sunny day was about to turn to rain, but there wasn't a cloud in sight.

How strange, she thought. Maybe it was a plane. But it would have to be a large plane—a large, fast plane.

Within minutes she had spotted Matthew. He was under the picnic table by himself.

"Hey, Matt," she called lightly as she reached for his hand. "Want to play on the swings?"

He eagerly took the pretty teacher's hand and came out from his hiding spot, putting both arms around her in a big hug.

"Oh, sweet little one, why are you all by yourself?" she asked, knowing he probably couldn't tell her as he was barely two years old.

She carried him over to a swing, gently placed him down, and began to push him from behind. Matthew felt safe, and then she began to sing, softly and sweetly, and he felt happy.

"Girls and boys, come out to play,
The moon doth shine as bright as day;
Leave your supper, and leave your sleep,
And come with your playfellows into the street.
Come with a whoop, come with a call,
Come with a good will or not at all.

Up the ladder and down the wall,
A halfpenny roll will serve us all.
You find milk, and I'll find flour,
And we'll have a pudding in half an hour."

After a while, Ms. Wolpert put him down and led him over to a small group of boys.

"Now you go have fun," she coaxed.

Recess was almost over, and they had made it through without any rain. Whatever had been in the sky was gone now and nothing but blue skies remained.

She looked at her watch and picked up a whistle—five more minutes, just enough time for Matthew to get to know those boys—but as she looked over, she could see he had already retreated back under the picnic table.

Oh well, she thought, there's always tomorrow.

The kids raced into three lines when she blew the whistle. It was time to go inside for art.

She quickly scanned the lines of children. Where was Polly?

And Matthew?

She looked back at the picnic table where she had just seen him a moment earlier. But he wasn't there. As she surveyed the lines again, she counted at least five children missing.

A slight wave of panic rose from her gut. They had to be hiding. She quickly summoned Mr. Dunkel, the principal, on her walkie-talkie.

He and a few other teachers came outside and together they looked under tables, in trees, behind playground equipment, but the kids were nowhere to be seen.

Ms. Wolpert's eyes widened with fear, and she tried her best to stifle the scream when she realized what had happened.

The kids had vanished.

A small group of children have been distracted by a strange man. Drawn into a secluded corner, out of sight from other adults, the children follow the man out of the schoolyard and into a waiting van.

All but one, a little boy not more than two who decides something doesn't feel right, and he runs. The feeling of dread, of sheer horror, begins to grow. Looking ahead there is a patch of flowers and a yellow house; if he can just get there he'll be safe.

But a rock hidden in the grass is steps away and he trips, landing on his knees. He looks up, sweat dripping onto his lips, unable to catch his breath.

His breathing is so labored, the thought of formulating a word seems impossible—but he tries with all his might and can feel it rising from his gut and rolling out of his mouth in a scream.

"Mom!"

Suddenly, a strong hand grips his shoulder, pulling him up from the ground.

The man is very tall and he manages to scoop the small boy up in one big arm while placing a soft, moist cloth gently over his face with the other arm.

He feels strange.

The intense fear and panic is giving way to a sleepy sense of well-being.

Both arms are around him now, snug, secure—but gentle.

As both suns rose in the sky, a cool breeze slipped through the open bedroom window, waking Tim from the nightmare.

Back to the Beginning

It had been two weeks since he had been home from the hospital after his encounter with the yellow-haired man, the one he heard went by the name Canary.

The school year loomed long without his best friend Luke to share it with. There had been no word about any of the missing. They were just gone.

As he lay in bed, he pondered just going back to sleep. At least then he wouldn't have to deal with the loss. But then again, sleep didn't offer much relief because of the reoccurring nightmare. It had gotten worse over the last few nights. More detailed and terrifying.

Nope, sleep wasn't where he would find comfort. The only thing that would give him peace was finding his friends. And he felt sure that meant finding the place called Earth.

Jennifer Torres lives and writes in a little beach town on the coast of Florida. She loves to write about fantastical lands, secret passageways, and doorways to magical places. A journalist for over fifteen years, she has also written a series of celebrity biographies for children and numerous articles for magazines, newspapers, and non-profit organizations. **The Briny Deep Mysteries** series is her debut into mystery fiction.

Read each title in The Briny Deep Mysteries

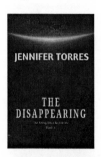

The Disappearing
The Briny Deep Mysteries Book 1

Tim and his four best friends learn that their quiet town of Briny Deep isn't as safe as they once thought. With children vanishing, they need to find answers before all their friends disappear.

ISBN: 978-1-62285-172-0

The Return
The Briny Deep Mysteries Book 2

The search for the missing children has now intensified. But when Tim seeks out the truth, he learns those closest to him have been keeping secrets from him. Briny Deep is no longer the place that Tim and his friends once knew.

ISBN: 978-1-62285-181-2

The Battle
The Briny Deep Mysteries Book 3

With the secret of Briny Deep finally exposed, Tim and his friends must travel far away to a strange land. And with a war between two distant worlds about to erupt, Tim must have the courage to dig deeper than he ever has before.

ISBN: 978-1-62285-186-7

CPSIA information can be obtained at www.ICGtesting.com
Printed in the USA
LVOW10s0735041014

407280LV00001B/5/P